DIRTY FILTHY RICH BOYS

LAURELIN PAIGE

PAIGE PRESS LLC

Copyright © 2017 by Laurelin Paige

All rights reserved.

No part of this book may be reproduced in any form or by any electronic or mechanical means, including information storage and retrieval systems, without written permission from the author, except for the use of brief quotations in a book review.

Dear Reader,

Welcome to your first glimpse of a whole new dirty, filthy world.

This free novella is actually the first section of Dirty Filthy Rich Men, book one in the Dirty Duet. Enjoy it and your first taste of Sabrina, Donovan, and Weston's story.

Before they were dirty, filthy rich men, they were dirty, filthy rich boys.

Pre-order Dirty Filthy Rich Men now, available March 27.

Also be sure to sign up for my newsletter where you'll receive a FREE book every month from bestselling authors, only available to my subscribers, as well as up-to-date information on my latest releases.

1

No one on earth could kiss like Weston King.

When his face lowered toward mine, my breath caught in the back of my throat. When his mouth met mine, electricity sparked. When his tongue slipped between my lips, I found heaven. My toes literally curled, just like the trite expression suggested. My heart pounded against my ribcage. Goose bumps stood up along my skin. Butterflies flitted in circles in my belly. Every cell, every *fiber* of my being felt his invasion. His kiss turned a body of flesh and blood and bone into something bigger. Something combustible. Something charged. Something aflame.

At least that's what I imagined his kisses were like.

My only evidence was based on observation, and, of that, I had plenty.

The girl he'd chosen to hook up with tonight definitely looked about to burst into flames with the way she was wriggling and writhing against him. Nichette? Was that her name? Or Nikita? It had been hard to hear her over the din of the party when she'd introduced herself to him an hour ago, and he'd only said it once or twice since then. It was something unusual and a bit pretentious and it blurred together with all the other unusual pretentious names of his previous hook-ups.

A guy I recognized from my economics class stumbled past, laughing with his buddies, and I pressed tighter to the wall, clutching my red Solo cup so it wouldn't spill. Though I didn't really care for whatever craft beer was on keg this week, it was one of my favorite things about the parties at The Keep. The main attraction was always craft beers and liquor. Most of the other rich Harvard students liked to draw crowds to their soirees with prescription drugs and recipes so experimental the FDA hadn't even had time to disapprove them yet.

The boys at The Keep kept things simple, and—except for a fair amount of underage drinking—legal. "*For those who might not want a blot on their past,*" I'd heard Brett Larrabee, the self-designated house manager, state on more than one occasion, usually when he was trying to convince a guy to suck his dick with his "one day I'm going to be a senator" pick-up routine. I had to give him credit—it usually worked.

My other favorite thing about the parties at The Keep was Weston King. It was actually the only reason I ever went to any of the shindigs. I was absolutely intrigued with him for no good reason other than that he was hot, charming and wealthy. He was my addiction. My obsession. My crush.

Gotta love hormones.

I'd noticed Weston on the first day of Intro to Business Ethics. I'd taken a seat in the front of the classroom (because I was that kind of girl), and he'd walked in late (because he was that kind of guy), smirking at something on his cell phone. The grin was still on his face as he tucked his phone in his back pocket, the glimmer still in his blue eyes. *Ice* blue eyes. The class was in a lecture hall, so it took him several seconds to cross the room, and I couldn't stop staring. I watched him the entire way. Watched him brush his hand through the dark blond hair that swooped over his forehead. Watched him give a wink to the teacher's assistant who was glaring at him for being tardy. This guy was confident. Cocky. Exactly like all the preppy rich kids who made it into Harvard because of significant monetary donations and a family name. He was the kid I wanted to hate, and I'd arrived in Cambridge with my scholarship and my father's lifetime savings wiped out planning to do exactly that.

But then his gaze crossed mine, and I don't even think he actually saw me, but I saw *him* and what I saw was fascinating. It was ease and charm and privilege and it made me buzz. Made me *breathe*. Made me blush with thoughts too dirty for an ethics class. It definitely made me forget every intention I had of hating his kind.

Instead, I wanted to know more.

It wasn't hard to find out about him. His father was Nash King, co-owner of King-Kincaid Financial, one of the world's largest investment firms, and without even having to ask, people talked about him. I soon discovered he was a freshman, like me, and that he lived with a bunch of guys in a four-story brownstone ten minutes off campus that had been passed among a few wealthy families for so long, no one remembered why they called it The Keep. The house was famous for the parties they threw every weekend. And though it was now late October and Weston had never once spoken to me or looked at me directly or even indicated that he knew I was alive, I'd come to every one.

Every time, I spent the evening in a corner watching him pressed up against some girl. Always a different corner.

Always a different girl. I'd tried to identify if he had a type, but I hadn't found a pattern. This one was a redhead. Last week was a blonde. The week before, the girl had almost exactly the same shade of brown hair as I did, but she was curvy. This redhead was as rail thin as I was, but she'd obviously purchased a set of breasts. Another time he'd been with a girl even flatter than I was. No pattern. No type. It led me to believe that all I'd have to do was get the courage to talk to him and then maybe...

But then what?

I wasn't delusional. I knew I had nothing special to offer. There was no trap that would set off the minute Weston's cock was inside me. He'd fuck me and be done. And then my obsession with him would be even more pathetic because I wouldn't just be a girl with a crush—I'd be a psycho who couldn't move on.

Still, I dreamt that I'd be different. That one day, he'd notice me and there'd be that spark and it would be the forever kind of spark and when he found out I'd been saving myself for someone just like him he'd want to work to earn me and he would. And it would be sweet and romantic and we'd live happily ever after.

For a business major, I'd always had a wild imagination. I was well aware.

"Hey, sexy!" One of the guys who lived in the house—I truly had no idea how many did—pulled a girl in a thigh-length sweater and printed leggings in for a hug, blocking my view. "Long time since I've seen you. Want to join in the next round?"

I circled around the pool table that the boys kept in place of a dining room table, squinting around people until I caught sight of Weston and his catch of the night. When I spotted them again, it was just in time. They were near the staircase and he was leaning in to whisper something into the redhead's ear. She responded with a giggle and then a nod.

This was it. The Exit. The moment the two of them would slip away to take things to The Next Level. The part that I spent the rest of the week imagining in fine detail—only, in my imagination, *I* was the girl, and very often, I accompanied the daydreaming with my hand beneath my panties.

Seriously, maybe I just needed to get laid.

I took another swallow of my not-so-delightful craft beer and cringed. Usually when Weston took off with his hook-up for the night, I finished up my drink and headed home. He would take her upstairs to his room now. At least, I guessed that's where his room was. The upper level was off-limits, the door to the stairway kept locked, and even if it wasn't, I wouldn't have ever intruded on their private space.

But this time when Weston and his catch went upstairs, he didn't shut the door tightly behind him. From across the room, my eyes focused in on the latch bolt sticking out from the doorframe, and something came over me. Something unexplainable. Because one minute I was standing against the wall like always and the next I was creeping in the shadows up the dark staircase to the top floor of The Keep.

The stairs were quiet and empty, and at the landing, I paused. The lights were off everywhere on the top floor, and it took a moment for my eyes to focus. There seemed to be a bathroom straight in front of me. To my right was a hallway, to my left was a bedroom with a door slightly ajar. Giggles drifted from the bedroom, and I tiptoed in that direction, cursing at myself every step of the way. What the fuck was I even doing? Was I planning to spy while Weston banged some other girl? Did I want him to suddenly notice me at the door and invite me in instead? Did I want him to invite me to *join*?

Yeah, this was messed up.

I nearly turned around.

I *should* have turned around.

But then Nicorette inhaled sharply and I had to know. Had to see.

I crept closer, peeked inside and nearly jumped when I saw the couple directly in front of me in a lip-locked frenzy. Then I realized that I was actually looking at a reflection in a wall-sized mirror. They were on the other side of the bed and the moon was shining in through the window illuminating the display.

And, oh my god, was it hot.

The redhead had already lost her shirt and her bra, and Weston was bent over her, suckling on one breast, kissing her pointed nipple while squeezing her other breast.

Nikita threw her head back and moaned. Unconsciously, I plumped my own breast over my sweater, and nearly gasped when I found my nipple sensitive and erect. I had to bite my lip to keep from making any noise. Had to cross my ankles to ease the throbbing between my legs.

I watched as Weston peeled off his shirt, the angle giving me a view of his beautiful, muscular back. He was on the rowing team. Of course. So preppy. So rich boy. But those muscles... God bless the rowing team.

And now he was undoing his jeans. And she was drawing out his cock. I could feel my eyes widen, trying to get a better look at his dick. I dared to lean in a little farther. Still, all I could make out was a dark shadow in the grip of the redhead's little palm as she stroked him up and down.

"Yeah, Nicky, just like that." The low rumble in Weston's

voice made my knees buckle. I could just hear him over the thump-thump of the bass drifting up from downstairs.

"It's Nichelle," she corrected. Right! That's what it was.

"Yeah, Nichelle." He pulled her head back up so he could devour her mouth. He kissed her for a few minutes, greedily, before pulling away and heading out of the reflection—toward *me*.

I cowered in the corner where the hinge met the frame, certain I was about to be discovered. But all Weston did was shut the door.

I leaned my back against the closed door and let out a deep breath.

Because what the actual fuck?

I could have gotten caught. I could have gotten kicked out of The Keep forever. I could have lost any respect Weston might have ever had for me before even earning it.

And why the hell was I so into this guy anyway? I didn't even *know* him! I needed to get my head in the right place. Needed to remember why my father put in all those years with the furniture store and why my mother's life insurance money was saved and put away. It was so I could go to the school of my dreams. Not so that I could spend all my time daydreaming over a pretty-faced playboy.

But what a pretty face he had.

God, I was in trouble.

"He's never going to go for you," a voice came out of the dark in front of me. "Not while you're a virgin."

I squinted, and when I looked closer, I saw there was another bedroom at the end of the hall with the door wide open, and though I couldn't quite make out the figure, I could see there was someone sitting in an armchair, smoking a cigarette. Or a cigar maybe.

I took a step forward. Surely he wasn't talking to me, but there didn't seem to be anyone else around. "Excuse me?"

"Weston never goes for virgins. It's one of his rules."

Heat rushed up my neck and flooded my cheeks. "Uh..."

"You're offended."

"Yes. I'm offended." And embarrassed. How long had this guy been watching me? It was pretty safe to assume that he'd seen me spying on Weston. Which was just...mortifying. Thank goodness it was too dark for him to see my face.

"Care to explain?"

I took another step forward. Then several more. Steps I should have taken down the stairs while I was still an anonymous girl in the dark.

But there was something about being watched privately by someone else that made me feel a kinship that I hadn't felt before. All that time I'd spent watching Weston, it was as though I'd been carrying a secret. And the first person to discover it had found it out by secretly watching *me*.

Or maybe that was just an excuse and I was just lonely. Or drunk. Or stupid.

"Well." I paused at the doorway of his room. "A of all, you can't possibly know what your roommate is and isn't into. And B of all, the status of my virginity is not something you can just presume."

He took a puff of his cigar—not a cigarette, it turned out —and the smoke filled the room with a sweet woody scent that reminded me of fireplaces and old libraries. "I beg to disagree. To both."

I huffed audibly. Because what else could I say to something as cocky as that?

Actually, plenty.

I threw my shoulders back, ready to go off when he went on first. "Look. I've known Weston since he was in diapers. I know him better than his mother does, I know him better than that girl who's in there currently sucking his dick, and I certainly know him better than you do."

He *did* know Weston well, I realized. I knew this guy, too. He was the T.A. for my ethics class. I hadn't recognized him at first, but now I did. He was Donovan Kincaid, son of Weston's father's business partner. I hadn't known he lived here. I'd never seen him at any of The Keep's parties before.

My hands started sweating and my pulse picked up a notch.

Donovan was several years older than us and was currently getting his MBA. He was a legend around campus because he was brilliant and ruthless. His business ideas were not only smart but also cutting edge. He was the sort of man who was going to rule the world. Tall, attractive, tough, powerful, strong. Perceptive. He intimidated me in general.

Right now? He scared the shit out of me.

"As for your virginity," he went on, "you wear it like a badge."

"I do not." I really kind of did. Right now, I was at a college party wearing a shapeless sweater and jeans. My hair was pulled into a loose ponytail. My shoes were Doc Martens that my roommate said had gone out of style a decade ago. It wasn't that I *tried* to be dumpy looking. I just liked to be comfortable. And as the older sister without a mother around, I'd never really had anyone teach me how to be a girl.

"There really is no reason to be offended," Donovan said, taking a sip from a glass. Whiskey, I was guessing. Something told me it wasn't his first glass of the night. "I'm not criticizing. In fact, I'm offering to help."

It took me a second to understand just what he meant. "Oh, please."

"I'm not kidding. Shall we discuss the pros and cons?"

I cocked my head and studied him, as if I could study him in the dark. Was he seriously offering to sleep with me? He obviously had no idea who I was.

"I, uh, don't think so." I tugged on the end of my ponytail, a nervous habit of mine. "I'm sure it's because there's no light in here or because there's so many of us in there, but I'm in your Intro to Business Ethics class. I'm your student."

He stretched to his side and yanked a chain, turning on a lamp next to him. I blinked several times in the newly lit bedroom. He wore a simple black sweater and jeans. His feet were bare. His unruly hair had more red in it in the dim light, his green eyes had more flecks of brown. It made him look more rugged than usual. More intense. His jawline added to the effect. It was lined with scruff, as if he hadn't shaved since class yesterday morning, and, though I'd never had such an impulse before, I found myself wanting to run my hand across the fuzz. Wanted to know exactly what it felt like under my skin. Was it soft? Did it scratch? Who was the last woman to run her hand across his jaw? Did he love her?

"I know who you are, Sabrina Lind." Donovan's declaration shocked me back to the here and now. "Ninety-seven point three average. You're here on a scholarship, so that matters. Never missed a day of class. Always sit in the front on the right side. Chad Lee cheats off your quizzes, but you don't know that. Your essays are on the detailed side but are creative, and I respect that. I appreciated your response to the unfair firing of Peter Oiler at Winn-Dixie Stores, but your perspective on Ford's decision not to modify the early versions of the Pinto was short-sighted."

My jaw dropped. There was too much to react to. I chose the easiest to respond to first. "Ford's decision killed people."

"It made the company money. It's called utilitarianism."

Even as he was heartless, his voice was smooth, like the fine scotch that I imagined lingered on his tongue.

I wondered briefly what it would taste like against my own tongue.

Just as quickly, I forced the thought out of my mind. "And I thought the class was called business *ethics*." The case he referred to had bothered me a lot. In 1970, Ford had discovered a major error with the Pinto that would likely cause several hundred deaths and injuries. Instead of fixing it however, their cost-benefit analysis determined it would be cheaper to settle the presumed lawsuits. So they didn't make the modifications.

"I think I've taught that ethics have to be personally defined." Donovan sat back and crossed one ankle over his knee. He searched my face before taking another puff of his cigar. "The offer still stands."

"What offer?" I blinked once before realizing which offer he meant. "Did you miss the part where you're my teacher?" And why was I still standing here talking to the guy? I should have left by now. But I was glued in place, fascinated with this discussion as I'd ever been with Weston King.

"I'm not actually your teacher. I'm the teacher's assistant." This was technically true. Mr. Velasquez officially taught the Monday, Wednesday, Friday class. But he only taught half of the time, and even when he did teach, Donovan still sat at his corner desk and graded papers or read or did whatever it was that he did while the rest of us listened to the lecture.

Apparently one of the things he did was watch us.

Or did he just watch me?

A string of goose bumps popped up along my skin at the

thought. I hugged myself and rubbed my hands up and down my arms.

Donovan's lip quirked up, as if he knew exactly the reaction he was having on me. "It's not officially against school policy if I fraternize with students."

I shook off a shiver. "By my own personal definition, it would be unethical."

"And why is that?" His voice wasn't just smooth, it was warm. Coaxing, even with its bitter edge.

"You grade my papers."

"So?" His stare was direct. Intense.

And this conversation was ridiculous. I wasn't considering it. Was I?

I glanced up, just to get my eyes away from him for one minute, and my gaze landed on a framed portrait on top of his fireplace. It was a picture of Donovan with a woman, both laughing as though they were caught candidly. It couldn't have been taken too long ago—Donovan looked nearly the same age as he was now, but his hair was short and clean-cut. And I'd never seen the woman. Maybe she was someone waiting for him back home. Or someone he'd broken up with. Or someone he was cheating on by flirting with me.

I looked back at him and realized he'd caught me looking at the picture. "If I fooled around with you, my scores might be affected," I said, answering his last question.

"If you *don't* fool around with me, your scores might be affected." His tone seemed hard now. Cold.

I smiled tightly and shifted my balance from the ball of one foot to the ball of the other, trying to decide if he was kidding.

His expression said he wasn't.

I swallowed. "You're an asshole."

"Am I? You're the one who came up here trying to get something from me."

"What do you mean?" The conversation had totally gotten away from me, and wherever it had gone, I was sure I didn't want to be there.

"You're alone with me in my bedroom. What else am I supposed to think you're after?"

A chill ran through me. The hair stood up on the back of my neck. The blood drained from my face.

Donovan set his drink down on the side table and leaned forward so his forearms rested on his thighs.

"Get out of here, Sabrina. This floor is off limits during our parties. Next time you attend one, maybe you'll think about the ethics of obeying house rules."

I turned around and dashed downstairs without hesitating another second.

2

I grabbed my coat from the bedroom on the main floor where everyone stacked their jackets and ran outside, tying my belt around my waist while I bounded down the front steps of The Keep. I pulled my phone from my pocket and looked at the time. It was too late to risk walking back to my apartment alone. It wasn't far, but this was campus territory, and I was a better-safe-than-sorry kind of girl. I used my app to arrange for an escort, put my phone away and then rubbed my hands together to keep warm.

It was a cold night. Fall set in right on time in Massachusetts. But like hell was I going back inside. I'd rather freeze.

Which was dumb. I was only punishing myself when I really wanted to punish Donovan. What the fuck was that anyway?

I replayed our entire conversation as I paced the front walk, trying to figure out exactly what had happened between us. All of it had been strange and borderline inappropriate, but there *had* been something else going on. Hadn't there? Something I couldn't quite put my finger on. I should never have engaged, wouldn't have engaged in a hundred other similar situations, yet I'd been drawn to him. He'd drawn me *to* him. That's the thing about Donovan Kincaid, the thing he was famous for—he was a known puppet master. He was a man who pulled the strings, and he'd pulled me to him.

Then why had he turned so icy at the end?

Obviously that was his game the entire time. He was messing with me. He caught me where I shouldn't be, and he made me pay for it. I deserved it. Didn't mean I liked it. And it definitely didn't mean I liked Donovan.

I glanced up at his window and shivered. Was he standing there right now? Watching me through the glass?

I could almost see the flare of his cigar in the dark. Could almost feel his eyes crawling along my skin. Imagining it made me feel both warmer and colder all at once. Like I was less alone and more alone than ever.

The front door of The Keep opened then, startling my attention in that direction. Theo, a guy I'd seen around a few times, ambled onto the porch and sniffed the air. "Fuck! It's cold as balls out here."

Ginger Baldwin followed out behind him with a guy that I guessed she was going home with based on the way they were hanging on each other. "Your balls are cold?" she asked with a giggle. "Is that a normal thing?"

"*My* balls aren't cold," her boyfriend of the night piped in, as if the idea would turn her off. "You've got a problem with your anatomy."

"Har har." Theo adjusted himself. "My anatomy is fine. Shall we whip them out and compare?"

"You're always trying to get me to whip it out. Are you sure you're not trying to tell me something?"

Theo huffed, angrily. "You know what? Fuck off."

I lowered my head and eased into the shadows on the side of the steps. Casual socializing wasn't my forte when all the participants were sober, much less when some were as drunk as these obviously were. I wasn't in the mood for talking to anyone at the moment, anyway.

Unfortunately, the movement must have caught Theo's eye. "Who's that over there?"

I pulled out my phone and pretended to be texting someone, pretended not to be listening to them, but I could feel their eyes on me.

"I know her. She's in my statistics class," Ginger said quietly. Then louder as she came down the stairs, "Hey, Bree. You okay?"

"Yeah." I pocketed my phone. "Just waiting for my escort." Like a loser. With no one to walk her home like the cool kids. I'd managed to drag my roommate to one of the early parties, but it hadn't been her scene. Besides, Sheri and I weren't that close, for no other reason than that our schedules didn't match up and she had a boyfriend who occupied her time.

Ginger smiled a little too widely, and I could imagine her thinking, *thank god, I didn't really want to deal with you, so I'm glad I don't have to,* while she kindly said, "Awesome. Glad you used the app." She followed her boyfriend to his car parked in front of the house.

Her escort, like a gentleman, opened the door for her, then called out to his friend still standing on the bottom step. "Theo, you coming?"

Theo ran both his hands through his hair and shrugged. "Nah, I'm going to walk." But instead of stepping down to the sidewalk, he strode over to me. "First, I'll look out for Sabrina while she waits. That's cool with you. Right, Bree?"

I didn't know the guy except from having seen him at

previous parties. The offer was odd and out of place. "It's really not necessary."

"That's a good idea," Ginger's date said, standing with the door open on the driver's side of the car. "Shouldn't be out here alone. You can never be too careful."

I wasn't alone. There was a whole houseful of people behind me and an escort on the way. But if Theo felt like a good scout to wait with me and if it gave Ginger and her guy an easy way to get rid of their third wheel, so be it. "Right. That's true. Thanks."

If Theo thought I was going to be chatty, though, he had another think coming.

The car had just barely taken off when I realized it wasn't chatting that Theo was interested in.

"Sabrina," he said, inching closer to me. Closer than I liked. "You're a lot prettier than you let on. I'm sure you get told that all the time, don't you?"

"No. I don't. Thank you, but." I pulled on the back of my ponytail and turned my head from him to look at the curb. The problem with the escort service was it was understaffed. Especially on Saturday nights. There was no telling how long it would be before it would get here. Maybe I should have waited inside after all. It wasn't too late to change my mind.

"Why do you hide all that pretty?" Theo reached his hand out and tugged at the belt of my coat, pulling it open.

"Excuse me?" I turned my head sharply toward him and yanked my coat back from him, but he wouldn't let go.

"I bet you have a gorgeous body too."

"Theo, thank you, but I'm uncomfortable with what you're saying. And what you're doing." He was drunk. That was all. He was just being playful.

Except he wasn't just being playful. He stepped closer. "I

don't really care if you're comfortable with what I'm saying, Sabrina." His breath smelled faintly of beer, but his words weren't slurred. He was in complete control of himself. He knew what he was doing.

I tried to step around him, but he put a hand up on the wall behind me. I had nowhere else to go. I'd made a mistake when I'd ducked into the shadows earlier because now I was in the corner where the stairs met the house, and Theo was blocking my escape.

"Theo. Please." I swallowed the ball at the back of my throat.

He sniffed, the second time I'd heard him, either from the cold or from snorting, I wasn't sure. "Please what?" he said as if he really didn't have any idea what I was asking.

"Let me go."

He feigned consideration then shook his head as if he was sorry he couldn't comply with my request. "Look." He pulled his thumb along my bottom lip, which quivered under his unwanted touch. "I don't want to draw this out, so here's how this is going to go—I'm going to fuck you. You can either make it easy or you can make it hard. Either way, we both know who has the power here."

I didn't even think. I just opened my mouth and started to scream. "Hel—!"

Theo was ready for me. He clamped his hand over my mouth—cutting me off before I could get any real sound out—and grinned from ear to ear. "I was actually hoping you'd choose the hard way. I like it when girls struggle. It will be better for you too. I'll come a whole lot faster."

"Fuck you," I said, muffled against his claw. And though I hated giving him what he wanted, though he was at least six feet tall and probably two hundred pounds, though I had no chance in hell at getting away from him, I fought back. I pushed against his shoulders with all my strength. I kneed at him. I wriggled. I cried.

Theo only chuckled. "Just like that, baby." He pressed his body in tighter against me, using his thighs to keep my lower body from squirming. With his free hand, he undid his pants and drew out his cock.

I started crying harder. I'd seen a penis before. I was a virgin but not a prude. I'd had a high school boyfriend. I'd given him blowjobs and handjobs and he had done enough to me in return that I wasn't even sure my hymen was still intact.

But looking at Theo's cock made me want to throw up. It had to be the ugliest thing I'd ever seen. Everything about it was disgusting. I didn't want it anywhere near me. Definitely didn't want it inside me.

I had to get out of this.

I brought my hands up to his face and scratched as hard as I could. Scratched until I drew blood.

Theo cursed and let go of his dick so he could wrestle my hands down instead. When he had them pinned tightly under my breasts, he moved his other hand so it covered my nose as well as my mouth.

"I can keep my hand like this, and in a couple minutes you won't have the energy to fight me. Would you prefer that, Sabrina? Is that the way you want to do this?" He locked his eyes right on mine, got right up in my face so he was sure I understood what he was saying. So he was sure that I understood that he was giving me the choice of whether or not he let me breathe.

I shook my head.

"So you'll be good?"

Did I have a choice? My lungs were already aching. My

eyes were already seeing spots. My brain was already panicking with the impulse to take a breath.

I nodded.

He didn't move his hand.

I nodded harder. I cried harder. Desperate.

Finally he moved his hand down ever so slightly so that my nostrils were uncovered. I inhaled cold air in long, sputtering draws, taking as much as I could get in through my nose. My chest rose and fell with each gasping breath.

Slowly, Theo let go of my hands, giving me another warning look as he resumed stroking his cock.

I got it. He had the power. I did not. Lesson learned. Lesson fucking learned.

I still struggled. I couldn't help it. It was like a reflex. Like that one time I'd gotten a pedicure and couldn't help kicking the technician because I was so ticklish. I willed myself to cooperate with Theo, and still my body fought him.

"Undo your jeans," he ordered after he'd jacked himself for a minute, his voice tight.

No. Please no, don't make me. I didn't move. I couldn't.

He inched the hand over my mouth slightly toward my nose—threatening—but I was already undoing the snap. Unzipping the zipper.

Tears leaked down my cheeks as Theo shooed my hands away. He licked two of his fingers and said, "Don't want to go in dry," then he stuck them inside my panties, searching for the hole he wanted.

A sob bubbled deep in my chest, and I closed my eyes, wishing I could be someplace else, surrendering to a deluge of mismatched thoughts that went on and on randomly. A panicked stream of consciousness. *I'm not here. I'm somewhere else. I'm on the beach. I'm in the Riviera Maya. I can't tell my father. He'll be so mad. I haven't shaved. Can you get frostbite in October? That redhead had nice breasts. What was her name again? It's just my virginity. It's just sex. Will I tell my sister? This is so embarrassing. I should have waited inside. It's so cold. Who was the blonde in that picture in Donovan's room? That last trip we took with Mom to the Riviera Maya was in October. It will be five years this December. What if he hurts me? What if he really hurts me? I hope no one comes out and sees this. I can't tell my sister. I can't tell anyone. Nichelle. I keep forgetting her name on purpose. I miss my mom. Please, God, let someone come and stop this!*

I was still aware of everything around me. Hyperaware. I knew I'd forever be able to identify the smell of Theo's shampoo. Of his cologne. His watch ticked in the quiet, each second sounding after an eternity while his fingernails scraped along the walls of my insides.

But I must not have been as attentive as I thought I was, because I never heard the door open or the footsteps on the stairs. I didn't see Donovan grab Theo by the back of his jacket and pull him off of me, but I did see him punch Theo squarely in the nose, heard it crack, saw the blood gush.

"What the fuck?" Theo howled, one hand holding his nose while he quickly pulled up his pants with the other. "Jesus, Kincaid!"

My knees nearly buckled in relief. I was free of Theo, free of his sweaty hand and his oppressive body. I scooted away from the corner I'd been trapped in, afraid I might somehow end up imprisoned there again, and fastened my pants as fast as I could. Shock halted my tears, and though I felt steady, I could see my hands were shaking.

Theo, seeming to see that he might be in trouble, took a step away, but Donovan grabbed his arm and yanked him back. "Did I say we were finished?" Theo had Donovan beat on size, yet Donovan didn't seem concerned at all.

I bit my trembling lip and hugged my arms around myself. Donovan might not be scared, but I was. Too scared to leave to get help. Too numb.

"Hey, I don't know what you think happened—" Theo started to say, but Donovan cut him off.

"You don't get to talk." Donovan yanked Theo's arm again. Hard. "It's up to Sabrina whether she presses charges. Sabrina?" Donovan looked at me, his green eyes searing into mine, searching as though he was afraid I was lost.

Maybe I *was* lost.

I blinked. He'd asked me a question. "What was that?" I managed.

"Do you want to press charges against Theo?"

The reality of the situation came crashing back on me full force. I'd been assaulted. That asshole had had his fingers inside me. If Donovan hadn't shown up, he'd have raped me by now.

I choked back bile.

Of course I wanted to press charges. Except...

I thought about it again. Went quickly through the scenario—white rich boy accused of assault by a nobody girl. Alcohol involved. No actual rape. Scholarship at risk. There was no way this would end in my favor, as much as I wanted it to. As much as the world needed brave warriors for violated women, it wasn't what I wanted for myself. It shamed me, but it was my truth.

"It's fine," I mumbled, a tear slipping down my cheek. I just wanted to forget all of this. Go home, take a bath. Pretend none of this ever happened.

"What?" Donovan asked, forcing me to repeat myself.

"I'm not pressing charges," I said louder. "I'm sorry." I didn't even know who I was apologizing to. Myself. Every victim of assault who'd never gotten a chance to face her attacker in cuffs.

"Fine." Donovan let go of Theo's arms, but when Theo turned around to face him Donovan kneed him in the nuts. "You deserve worse, you asshole. Unfortunately, the U.S. legal system probably wouldn't give you much more than that. Penalties at The Keep are more severe though. You're not welcome here. You won't do business with our families. Your investments at King-Kincaid will be canceled. Now get the fuck off my property. You're bleeding all over my Ferragamos."

Theo wiped the blood dripping from his nose with the back of his hand and leaned a shoulder forward as though he were going to challenge Donovan. Then he seemed to think better of it and took a step backward. "All right. All right, Kincaid. Didn't realize you were saving this one for yourself."

"Get the fuck out of here." Donovan never raised his voice, but his tone and his eyes and his posture said it all. Theo took off.

I was still shaking, still crying. I swiped the tears from my eyes and started to turn to thank Donovan when a car pulled up to the curb. I turned my attention there instead. It was my escort. What timing.

When I shifted back to Donovan, he was already climbing back up the stairs toward the front door without a goodbye. Without even an, "Are you all right?"

I cried the entire drive home. Cried for an hour in the shower. It wasn't until hours later when I was curled up in the fetal position in my bed that I realized that Donovan's Ferragamos were boots. And they'd been tied. He'd seen my situation through his bedroom window then taken the time to lace them up before coming downstairs to rescue me.

3

I didn't go to classes on Monday.

I said I had the flu and stayed in bed, facing the wall. Sheri brought me microwaveable soup and crackers from the Shell station, and I told her I was only crying because my head hurt.

Tuesday, I managed to pull myself together. Nothing happened, really. Theo hadn't actually raped me. I was the same girl I'd been before. It wasn't like I had to see him again either. I didn't have any classes with him. He was an upperclassman, and we didn't run in the same circles. And no one else knew what had happened—I'd decided not to tell a soul—so all I had to do was smile and pretend nothing had happened. Easy peasy.

If it wasn't exactly easy, it was at least doable. As doable as it had been when my mother had died five years ago and kids at school had pointed and whispered behind my back. I'd put on a happy face and acted as if it meant nothing. As if it didn't hurt. That experience with tragedy had taught me an important lesson in how to deal with hard things—you smile, you nod, you go on.

That's how I'd planned to handle Intro to Business Ethics too. I knew it would be different because of Donovan, because he knew. But it wasn't like he was going to bring it up in class. We'd never even talked before that night at The Keep. He was my teacher. I looked to him to learn things. He looked at me as another paper to grade. I didn't think it would be a problem.

I walked in to the lecture hall, early as usual, and headed for a seat in the front row. Normally I came in from the door below, but this time I came in from above since I'd stopped for a bottle of water before class and taken a different route to get there. As I walked down the stairs, I glanced down at the teacher's desk, and maybe I was a little nervous about seeing Donovan because I silently hoped it was Velasquez teaching today.

It wasn't.

Donovan sat at his laptop, wearing his grey trousers and a dress shirt and tie under his black pullover, and as though he could sense me, he looked up just then and caught my gaze.

I froze, unable to take another step.

My knees swayed. Sweat beaded on my brow. It was like he was a trigger. My entire pretense fell apart, and I was transported back to that night. I swore I could feel Theo's palm across my mouth. The sound of his nose cracking echoed in my ears. Emotion overwhelmed me.

But it wasn't just terror and humiliation that I felt. There was something even worse underneath it all. Something ugly but undeniable.

As soon as I recognized it, I flushed with panic. Donovan had to notice because his eyes narrowed and his chin tilted up with curiosity. I wanted to turn around and run out of the classroom, but that would only direct attention to myself. Besides, my legs felt like jelly at the moment, so I slipped into a seat in the row I was already standing in and ducked my head, pretending not to realize that my behavior might be odd or that he was still watching me.

Actually, I wasn't pretending—I didn't *care* if he was watching me. I didn't even care about keeping an eye out for Weston like I usually did. I had to figure out what the everliving fuck was wrong with me. My heart was pounding, my clothes felt too hot, I felt restless and unsettled.

But it wasn't thoughts of Theo that had me riled up. It was Donovan. From the way he'd taunted me in his bedroom to the way he'd commanded the situation with Theo to the way his jaw set when he studied me with those intense eyes.

God, those eyes...

I snuck a glance at him as he stood up to start the lecture, and another tumultuous, confusing wave rolled through my body. I shifted in my seat, but it didn't help. When he started talking it was even worse. His voice sent shivers down my spine. I drank in every word, yet sentences went by without me comprehending a single phrase.

I was seriously fucked.

Whatever was happening, there had to be a perfectly natural explanation. Like, I was having a psychotic break. My mind was trying to change the terrible thing that happened to me by associating Donovan and pleasant feelings with that night instead of Theo and those awful ones.

Except these feelings weren't exactly pleasant. They were sick and tormenting. They were fierce and turbulent. I had to cross my legs and uncross them at least a hundred times just to make it through his lecture, the whole time hating myself because I couldn't settle down.

It all made me mad. And uncomfortable. And then mad

again. For so many reasons. I was mad at Donovan anyway because of everything he knew. Not just about what Theo did, but those other things that he'd said about me in his room. Those things he'd perceived about me so easily. I didn't like him knowing me like that. It felt invasive. Like a violation.

And I was mad about how he'd taken his time in rescuing me.

And how he didn't even seem to really be sure he was glad he saved me at all.

Mostly I was mad about the thoughts I was having about him, even though they weren't really his fault. Yet, if he hadn't been so fucked up with the way he'd gone about dealing with that night, I wouldn't probably be so fucked up with the way I felt about it now. So maybe it was fine to blame him for that too.

Whoever was to blame, it didn't matter. I was the one who had to deal with it. It wasn't like he cared about how I'd come out of the nightmare. I'd figure it out, somehow.

After what felt like the longest hour of my life, the class was finally over. I took off the second we were excused, careful to dodge Donovan by going up the stairs again instead of exiting below. I'd planned to grab lunch with a friend, but I had to run by my apartment first to change my panties before my next class. That's how bad it was.

Once I was out of Donovan's presence, I was sure the whole strange thing would blow over. I thought about Weston to clear my head. He was the guy I'd been into. He was the one that gave me butterflies to think about. Still. Even now.

The rest of the day, however, I found my mind wandering back to Donovan now and then, found myself imagining different endings to the night at The Keep. What if he had asked me back inside after Theo had left? What if I hadn't left his room in the first place?

I was ashamed of myself.

But it's where I got the idea of how to deal with the bad dreams I'd had ever since it had happened. That night when I woke up in a cold sweat with the ghost of Theo's touch on my skin, I slid my hand beneath my panties and erased the memory with thoughts of Donovan.

"Did he hurt you too badly?" he asked, cupping my cheek as Theo hobbled down the street. His hand was warm against my skin, tentative without being gentle.

"Not too badly," I whispered, looking into his hazel eyes. My escort pulled up at the curb and both of us turned toward it, but instead of walking away, Donovan pulled me into his arms.

"Let me take care of you tonight." With a nod, he sent the car away. Then he bent to his knees and pulled down my pants, pulled down my underwear, neither asking permission nor apologizing for his eagerness.

But I wanted him there, so it was different than when Theo had forced me.

The air was cold on my bare legs, but soon all I felt was the heat of his tongue between my folds. He licked up and down my slit aggressively several times, then thickened his tongue to a point and inserted it inside me.

I came almost at once and slept soundly until morning.

Whatever it was that Donovan did to me didn't go away but I got better at dealing with it. I learned not to look him in the eye. I stopped sitting in the front row in class. I did what I always did—I smiled, I nodded, I went on.

And at night, I continued to soothe my dreams with fantasies of him fingering and fucking me, usually in some strange version of my assault. Sometimes it would happen after he'd pulled Theo off me. Sometimes Theo wasn't there at all. Sometimes I asked him to. Sometimes I begged.

And sometimes—a lot of the time—he was as callous and cruel as Theo had been.

4

"Sorry about that."

"No—" I did a double take at the guy who'd bumped into me as he was getting into the seat next to me. Weston King. "—problem," I finished.

I sat up straighter in my own chair and glanced down at what I was wearing. Jeans. Sweater. Ponytail. Boring. Ugh. Well, what did I expect? It was kind of hard to hide from someone like Donovan while still trying to be noticed by someone like Weston. Both were impossibilities, I'd decided in the three weeks since the Theo incident, because it seemed I always saw Donovan and Weston never saw me.

Until today when, miracle of miracles, Weston happened to take a seat next to me.

My heart was pounding a thousand beats a minute, my knee couldn't stop bouncing. Eep! Our elbows were practically touching. Then there was the added glee I had when he pulled out a spiral notebook from his bag. He was a boy who took notes old-school style! Swoon!

This was almost enough of a delight to distract me from the lecture Donovan had been giving before Weston had arrived. Unfortunately, the former still had a pull on me that I couldn't deny. Especially when he was addressing issues that got me worked up such as the one he was tackling today—deregulation in the financial industry.

I'd come a long way on this topic in my short time at Harvard. While I could see the hurdles and obstacles that regulation put on investment firms such as King-Kincaid, I was still a girl who came from the other side. It wasn't the billionaires losing their pensions during the Great Recession. It wasn't the rich having their homes and cars and lives taken away from them. Regulation was how ethics were implemented, as far as I was concerned, and I'd said as much in as many ways as possible in my last paper.

As much as I believed in regulation, I knew that, as always, my annoyance at Donovan had less to do with what he was preaching and more to do with what he did to me in my thoughts on a daily basis in the bedroom. What he was doing even now, as much as I hated to admit it, drawing me to him. Commanding my attention. Demanding my focus.

Damn, I hated him.

"Fuckwaffle," I said under my breath.

Weston shifted in his seat next to me. "What did you say?"

Oh my god. My face went red. "What?"

He leaned in close so I could hear him without disturbing the class. "Did you just call Kincaid a fuckwaffle?"

"I shouldn't have said that." But if that's what it took to have Weston lean in to whisper in my ear then I'd consider saying it again. Maybe. After my embarrassment died down. Like, in the next century.

"Don't take it back!" Weston exclaimed quietly. "That's awesome! I love it."

I spun my head toward him. "Aren't you guys friends, or...?" Man, his eyes were even bluer this close up. And he had freckles—light ones—along his nose.

"More like family, and I love him like a brother. But he's a total fuckwaffle." His brow rose. "And I don't think I've called him that yet. Do you have a pen I could borrow?"

"Uh...yeah." I dug in my bag searching for one.

Weston peered over my shoulder. "That one. That Sharpie would be awesome."

We grabbed it simultaneously, our fingers brushing, and I had to bite my lip not to gasp.

"Thanks," he said, smiling just enough to show that wicked dimple. Jesus, I could fall inside that dimple and never crawl back out. That dimple was going to be the death of me.

I watched as he flipped through his notebook. The pages had single words written across them, all landscape. *Tool, Shitstick, Asshat, Douchebag, Buttmunch, Jizztissue.* He stopped on a blank page and took the top of the black Sharpie off with his mouth. I was seriously going to make out with that Sharpie lid later. Then he started writing: *Fuck*—

"What are you doing?" I asked, suddenly both nervous and excited like I was about to be privy to something that might be a little bit bad but not so bad that words like *expulsion* or *policeman* could be brought up. The kind of bad that always seemed like it might be fun but also might be addictive.

"I always write notes for Donovan when he teaches to let him know how he's doing. *Fuckwaffle* is not a note I've given him before." When he finished writing the word, he held up the notebook as if he was scoring an event.

I was seriously giddy. "And you do this every class?"

"When Velasquez isn't here. Well, sometimes when he is

here I try to sneak in a note too." Some other students in the row across the aisle flagged Weston so he'd show them today's note.

How had I missed this before today?

Weston brought the notebook back in front of him and waved it around a few more times for Donovan, who didn't even blink in our direction. If we were sitting farther up in the hall, I'd wonder if he could read it, but we weren't that far from the front and the black Sharpie made it pretty clear.

Genius.

"Does he ever acknowledge you?" I asked, amazed at how stoic Donovan remained.

"Nope." Weston closed the notebook and tucked it back into his bag. "It never gets old either. I must have a nine-year-old's sense of humor or something. It's like when you go to Buckingham Palace and try to get the guards to smile, you know?"

The farthest place I'd ever been from home was here. Even our one family trip to Mexico had been closer. "I've never been to Buckingham Palace."

He looked at me then, really looked at me. Judged me, maybe, for never having been to England—the most basic of rich people places in the world. Did that matter to a guy like him?

A smile eased across his full lips. *Ah, that dimple.* "Then I'll have to take you there." He leaned close again and tugged my ponytail. "I'm Weston."

I almost forgot how to breathe. "I know who you are. I come to your parties." Or I used to. "I'm Sabrina."

Almost simultaneously as I introduced myself, my name rang out across the hall in Donovan's baritone timbre. "Sabrina. Care to share your thoughts on regulation and ethics? I know you have quite a few."

My stomach dropped. I hated talking in front of a class, but more importantly, Donovan never called on students. *Never.* What the hell was his problem? We weren't the first kids to be caught chatting during his lecture, surely.

"Fuckwaffle," Weston whispered next to me, sending me into a fit of nervous giggles.

Thankfully, Donovan noticed the time. "Saved by the figurative bell. It looks like class is over." The resentment in his tone was thick. "Grades for your corporate strategy and ethics awareness assignment will be on the portal by the end of the week. Remember this thesis will count for half your grade." He seemed to be staring at me as he said this, most likely because he was still sore that I'd disrupted his lesson.

I scowled. I hated it when he looked at me like that, but I wondered right then if I'd miss it if he suddenly stopped. I had a feeling I would.

I wondered if he'd miss it if I stopped staring back.

"Do you have another class now?" Weston asked.

I pulled myself away from Donovan's piercing gaze and found Weston holding my bag out for me. "Thank you. And nope. Break until two." I shuffled into the aisle after him. "You?"

"I usually meet up with a friend for lunch."

I nodded. I'd thought for a moment he was going somewhere with his questioning. Guess he was just being polite.

But then he cocked his head in my direction. "Join us?"

∼

THE FRIEND, it turned out, was Brett Larrabee. I'd been

aware of Brett from the parties at The Keep, but we'd never officially met, and I was glad for the introduction. An extremely extroverted, politically conservative, openly homosexual African American, Brett was an oxymoron, and I found him absolutely intriguing.

He was also quite a talker. He'd led us to a small Vietnamese café, that was surprisingly not busy considering how good the food was, and proceeded to monopolize the majority of the conversation while we ate.

I didn't mind. I was happy just to be included on the excursion. Every few minutes I had to remind myself I was awake, that this wasn't a dream. That I was actually sitting at a table making a fool of myself with chopsticks in front of Weston King.

"The DOW is down, the DOW is down, the DOW is down," Brett said with weary distress as he scrolled through his financial app on his phone. Even though he talked a lot, he still managed to eat the fastest. He'd finished and had been playing on his cell for the last five minutes. "The Fed better not raise interest rates. It is not the time."

"Dad says it's coming soon," Weston said, pushing away his plate.

"Oh!" Brett's head popped up with the news of something he'd just remembered. "Did you hear about Theodore Sheridan?"

Theo. I dropped my sticks at the mention of his name. Fortunately, I'd dropped them so many times, no one noticed. Hopefully no one noticed my hands shaking as I took a sip of my water, my throat suddenly dry.

Weston considered a minute. "Nothing interesting I can think of."

Then you didn't hear the one where he almost raped a girl in front of your own porch? At least it was reassuring to know that Donovan hadn't told all his roomies. Not that I'd thought he was much of the sharing type.

Brett bent over the table and lowered his voice. "He got busted with more than a kilo of coke."

"And you're just mentioning this now?" Weston asked, as if reading my mind. Maybe Theo wasn't a close enough friend for him to consider it headline news, but it was to me.

That wasn't something I cared for anyone to know, though, so I kept my head low, scooting noodles around in my bowl. I'd lost any appetite that remained the minute I'd heard his name.

"Huh," Weston said, running his hand through his hair. "I knew he had a problem with blow, but what the fuck was he doing to draw attention to himself?"

"I don't know, but he was charged with intent to *sell*."

"Theo doesn't need money. He got his entire trust fund at eighteen."

"He's saying it's all cooked up charges or something. Whatever. Daddy Sheridan will get him off, but he's out for the year here."

"Crazy."

While it was a relief to think that Theo wouldn't be around anymore, I didn't get too excited by the thought that he'd face any prison time. Brett was right—his money and his privilege would get him off. Whether it was drugs or rape, he had the get out of jail free card.

Brett, seeming to be done with the Theo scandal, was ready for other gossip. "Did Numbnuts teach today?" he asked, leaning his chair back onto two legs.

"Actually," Weston said, raising a brow in my direction, "it was Fuckwaffle."

"That's a nice one." Brett turned his admiration to me. "You don't like Donovan? I have to hear this."

Did I like Donovan? What a loaded question. My emotions where Donovan was concerned were like paperclips—I couldn't pick up one without several others coming with it. I was grateful to him and resentful. Angry and preoccupied.

It wasn't something I could begin to explain to myself, let alone someone I'd just formally met. Tugging on my ponytail, I tried to think like a typical disgruntled student. "He's just...you know. A pompous, egotistical know-it-all. What about you guys? You live with him."

Weston exchanged a glance with Brett. "That we do. And like I said, I love him like a brother. But sometimes brothers are hard to love. Do you have one?"

It was a smooth change of subject, one I wasn't about to contest. Brett went back to playing with his phone, so I focused my answer just to Weston. "I have a sister. Audrey. But she's easy to love. She's thirteen and awkward and adoring."

Weston sat back in his chair, crossed his arms over his chest, and crossed his legs at his ankles. "She probably puts her eighteen-year-old sister up on a pedestal."

"Seventeen," I corrected.

"Seventeen?"

"I graduated high school early."

"Kudos. That's impressive."

"Thank you." I averted my eyes, embarrassed by the compliment, and sighed. "I'm still not sure I did the right thing deciding to come to school so far away from home."

"Where are you from?" he asked and it almost felt like more than small talk, like he really wanted to know.

"Colorado, but it's not really the distance that's the thing. It's that my mother died when I was twelve, and I feel bad leaving my dad and Audrey alone." I knew he probably didn't get it. He was from a world of nannies and chauffeurs and housekeepers and tutors. There was no such thing as alone. "What about you? Do you have siblings? Not like Donovan, but blood related?"

He'd started nodding before I'd finished the question. "I have a sister. She's ten, and we're in completely different worlds." He puckered his lips as he thought, which was ridiculously unfair, since I was already on hormone overload. "I really grew up closer to Donovan, even though he's four years older than me. We went to the same school, were on the same chess teams. We row together. Our families vacation together. I've always had him to look up to." He sat up straighter, leaning in as if confiding in me. "I guess I idolized him growing up."

"But not now?"

"It's different now."

He let that hang, and I searched for the right words to prod further while, at the same time, trying to understand exactly *why* I wanted to know more—because the answer said something about Weston? Or because it said something about *Donovan*?

I decided not to prod.

But then Brett said, "He's not the same since Amanda died. I'm a sophomore, so I didn't know him very long before that."

"Amanda?" Okay. I was definitely interested.

"Brett—" Weston warned.

Brett glared at him in return. "What? Are we not allowed to talk about it ever? He's not even here."

Weston paused for a beat. "Amanda was Donovan's girlfriend. She died in a car accident a year ago. Around this time of year. Coming back to school after Thanksgiving, actually."

The air left my lungs. "Oh my god! What happened?"

"Another driver didn't check his blind spot. He drove into her lane and pushed her into oncoming traffic. They said she died instantly. She was closer to campus when it happened, so it was Donovan who had to identify her body."

"That's awful. I feel awful." It was the kind of thing I'd say after hearing any sort of tragic tale, but I really meant it right now in a way I usually didn't. In a way I couldn't explain.

"They were the real deal, too," Weston went on. "He wanted the house, the kids, the whole nine yards. He'd planned to ask her to marry him for Christmas. I think he might have even bought her the ring."

She had to be the blonde in the picture on his mantle. He'd seen me looking at it just before he'd turned cold.

"Is that why he's so...?" I searched for the word I was looking for. What was it exactly that Donovan was? Distant? Cut-off? Alone?

Weston seemed to get what I meant. "He wasn't ever what I'd call friendly before that, but he's harder now. Sharper too. In some ways I think he's become a better businessman, if that makes sense."

"I think it does. It's like when you lose one sense and so your others become more acute." I had my mother's death to draw on as experience, but it was my assault that I was thinking of now. How had I changed since then? Was I harder or sharper or more business savvy?

And what about the thoughts I had at night now, the dirty thoughts with Donovan?

"Yeah. Like that," Weston said as the waiter set down the check.

I reached for my bag, but Weston shook his head. "No, I've got this." He dimpled at me as he handed his card off.

"Thank you. That's really nice." It came off halfhearted, though, because I was still thinking about Donovan. I was pained by his pain, for whatever foolish reason. He certainly hadn't shown any concern for mine. But more interestingly, I was *fascinated* by his pain. I could imagine how he carried it, where he stuffed the details of his misery. Inside this bottle of scotch. Under that heartless remark. Behind this wall of indifference.

He knew the secret I hid behind smiles and nods, and now I knew the agony he hid behind ice and steel.

Maybe we were finally even.

"Well," I said, forcing my attention back to Weston, "you sound like you've been a good friend to him."

"Because I give him notes as he lectures in class?" His tone was sarcastic, but I heard the hint of helplessness underneath. He really didn't know how to help his friend, his brother.

It wasn't like I had the answers, but at least I could reaffirm him. "Exactly because of that."

He looked up from the credit card slip he'd just signed and studied me. "Sabrina, I think you did the right thing coming to Harvard. I'm sure your dad will do just fine with your sister. He seems to have done a great job with you."

I chuckled dismissively. "You don't even know me."

"Sure I do. I know that you're strong. That you're resilient. That you're smart—probably smarter than both Brett and me. You're obviously beautiful." He reached over to tug my ponytail. "And I know that you're coming to my party on Saturday with me."

The butterflies were back, though they were flying now as though they had pebbles for wings. This was everything

I'd wanted, everything I'd hoped for. A date with Weston King. And all the murky, confusing feelings going on inside right now were probably just related to going to The Keep for the first time since Theo.

Yeah, that had to be it.

So. *Smile. Nod.* "I guess you do know me after all."

But how could he when I was only just starting to figure me out for myself?

5

Audrey: Dad won't make stuffing if you aren't here.

Me: Then make the stuffing yourself.

I moved my eyes from the chat box in the corner of my computer screen back to the Excel spreadsheet I was working on for Statistics. It was early Thursday afternoon, two days before Weston's party, one day after he'd invited me to go with him, and I was still vacillating between so many emotions about it that all I felt now was anxious. My sister's efforts to try and get me to buy a last minute flight home for Thanksgiving were not helping.

Another message popped up.

Audrey: But I don't know hoowwww!!!!

Like a true teenager, my sister was as dramatic in her chats as she was in any conversation.

> Me: You're 13. Stove Top is cinch.
>
> Audrey: But who's going to put olives on their fingers and make olive monsters with me?

A notification showed up on the top of my laptop saying I had a new item in the Academic Portal.

> Me: Put olives on Bambi.

Okay, Bambi was the dog. But seriously. I had homework to do. And homework to follow up on.

I clicked over to the Academic Portal and found that the new addition was to my Intro to Business Ethics folder. My corporate strategy and ethics awareness assignment that Donovan had said would be up this week. I opened up the scores and grades document and waited for it to load.

> Audrey: Very funny. Come hommmmmeeee!!!!
>
> Me: Aren't you in class right now or something?

I hit return and then froze. There, on my screen where my **A** should be there was a big fat **F**.

No way.

Not possible.

I'd never gotten an F in my life.

I opened up the remarks for details. *Student's conclusions disregard the corporation's economic responsibilities to its stockholders. Student speaks of moral high ground with poetic sentiment without considering how suggested actions will be funded. The student does not have a firm grasp of the concept of corporate strategy.*

Goddamn, Donovan.

All I could see was red. I understood the concept of corporate strategy. It was Donovan who couldn't understand the concept of an opposing opinion.

And this wasn't just my pride hurt. This counted for more than half the class grade. I wouldn't be able to get higher than a **D** if this wasn't changed and my scholarship required a **B** average.

No. Whatever beef Donovan had with me, he couldn't fuck with my grades.

Within a couple of minutes I'd looked up Velasquez's office hours and found that he should be available for another hour. The weather was great for November—there hadn't been any recent snow. I could make it if I hurried. If he looked over it, I was certain he'd see that my paper deserved to be re-graded and that Donovan was a fucking asshole.

The chat window dinged again.

Audrey: It's study period.

Me: I have to talk to you later, Audrey.

I closed my laptop and headed across campus to fight for my grade.

∼

THIRTY-FIVE MINUTES LATER, I stood outside Velasquez's office. I'd tried to calm myself down on the walk over so that I could present all my points rationally to my teacher, but instead, I'd just gotten more worked up. The paper had been fifteen pages long. I should have gotten a C just for turning in the required length. As for my disregard to shareholders—I'd attached a detailed financial plan. If my math had been wrong, that should account for a point or two, but not entire letter grades.

It was obvious this wasn't about my work—this was about Donovan. Why was he doing this to me? Part of me wondered if I should be going to The Keep instead, if it should be *his* door I should be banging on.

No. I wasn't playing games. Velasquez would fix my grade and if Donovan got in trouble for giving me a bad score then he deserved it.

The door was closed, but I could see the light on through the frosted glass. I knocked and bounced my hip impatiently while I waited for my professor to respond.

"It's open."

I turned the knob and stepped into the office. It was the size of a shoebox, lined with mismatched library-style bookcases, so cramped that the door wouldn't open all the way, and I had to shut it behind me to see Velasquez's desk.

Then, *fuck*, it was Donovan sitting behind it in his place.

Goddammit all to hell.

The son of a bitch didn't even look up from his laptop. "How can I help you, Sabrina?"

My hands were shaking. I stuffed them into my coat pockets. I couldn't talk to Donovan. Not like this. Not when he'd already written me off. "Where's Velasquez?"

"You have to schedule an appointment to see him." His dress shirt was crisp white and his muscles bulged tightly against the fabric.

I'm not looking at him. "I'd like to do that then."

"You can schedule online through the portal."

Jesus. Of course.

I put my hand on the doorknob, ready to leave.

"He's here on Fridays at three," Donovan said to my back.

I did a mental scan of my schedule. "I have class then."

"Then you'll have to skip class. Or you'll have to talk to me." Finally, he looked up at me—caught me, *caged* me with those sharp, piercing eyes. "What can I help you with, Sabrina?"

I didn't want to talk to him. And I didn't want to leave.

"My grade," I said.

He cocked his head, as if he had no idea what I meant, that asshole motherfucker. "What about it?"

Anger gave me courage. I pulled my hands out of my pockets and stepped toward him. "It's not fair, and you know it. I understand that you don't agree with my conclusions, but my reasoning was fair and sound, and I referenced many credible and reliable sources—"

He nodded to the chair facing the desk. "Sit down, Sabrina. You're awfully worked up."

He didn't even ask me to sit. He *told* me. It was patronizing and infuriating. "I'd like to stand." I was getting hot, though. I unbuckled my pea coat and threw it on the chair instead. "My paper was not 'F' work."

He nodded and ticked his jaw a couple times as though considering. After a beat, he said, "I care to differ."

"This is not subjective!" I yelled.

"It is, actually." His tone remained composed, in perfect contrast to mine. "Unfortunately, for you, it's my opinion that matters."

God, the calmer he was the more worked up I got. He was goading me on purpose. I should leave. I knew I should leave.

I started for my coat then stopped. "*Why* are you doing this?"

"It's sad, really." Donovan shut his laptop and pushed it aside. Then he clapped his hands together silently as if praying and pointed them at me. "You showed such promise at the beginning of the term, Sabrina. But this last month you've become a different person. You've arrived late to class. You're disengaged. You're disruptive. The work you're turning in—this paper—is less than acceptable. It's a shame you're letting the events of one night stain the rest of your life."

His last sentence was heavy and weighted with subtext.

"Are you—?" I was incredulous. Was he *really* blaming this on what happened with Theo? "Oh, and you're a perfect example of how not to let a tragedy stain the rest of your life."

His brows furrowed. "What did you say?"

Besides, I hadn't changed because of *Theo*. I'd changed because of *him*. Not that I was telling him that. "My changes in behavior have not translated into a change in the standard of my work."

"As your teacher, that's for me to decide, and I've decided

that it has." His subtext said *case closed*. Especially when he leaned back in his chair and rested his feet on the desk, crossed at the ankles.

Weeks of bottled up emotion rattled through me. Every cell in my body vibrated with rage and want and horror and shame.

"Fuck you," I said in as clear and as controlled a tone as I could manage. I'd leave. I'd talk to Velasquez. I'd report the fuck out of Donovan. I had a solid case. This wasn't even anything to worry about. I'd get it worked out.

I grabbed my coat off the chair and spun once again to leave.

"Don't you mean *fuckwaffle*?"

I'd had the door open, was *this close* to walking out, but I shut it again because I had to know. "Is *that* why you're doing this? Because of Weston?" Was he *jealous*?

For half a second, I thought I'd hit onto something. His expression tightened and a strange prick of heat blossomed in my belly at the idea of Donovan jealous. Because of *me*.

But then he laughed, coldly. "No. I was just teasing you. Can't take being on the other side of the joke?"

Is that what this was to him? A joke?

"This is serious!" I was so mad I dropped my coat and pushed his fucking feet off the desk. "This is my scholarship!"

In an instant he was up and around the desk in front of me. "I told you before how you could fix your grades if you're that concerned about it."

He was referring to his come-on in his room. When he'd suggested he could *help me* with my virginity. It was another way he could trivialize my situation, but it was also a chance to play with my emotions. I hated how it felt like a carrot dangling. How he played that card as if he knew that somewhere deep down I wanted him.

It pissed me off to a new level. I slapped him so hard my palm burned.

Donovan rubbed his cheek, and his eyes sparked. "Is this how you fought off Theo?" he asked, evenly.

"No," I said tentatively.

Something shifted between us.

"Fight me like you fought him."

I could have said no. It was such a strange, twisted request, but I was mad and ready to fight. And after weeks of the thoughts I'd had, weeks of pent-up desire and need, I didn't *want* to say no.

And was it really a strange, twisted request if somewhere on a gut level I understood the impetus behind it?

Without further urging, I shoved both arms against Donovan's chest as forcefully as I could. He pushed my hands away, but it felt good. Both to shove and be shoved. Like being able to pick up a heavy weight and the relief after you put it down.

Donovan nodded, encouraging me to come at him again.

I shoved him once more, but he grabbed my arm and wrapped it around my back. He tried for my other arm. I kneed him in his side then pushed against his face while he was bent over. He was too strong for me, and he captured my wrist easily.

He held me like this for a second as we caught our breath, all the while his eyes glued to mine. "Do you want me to stop?" he asked carefully.

Why wasn't I frightened? I was trapped by a man I didn't have any reason to trust, and I'd been in a similar situation and been violated. I should have been scared out of my mind.

But instead of feeling scared, I felt empowered.

And turned on.

Just like in all those fantasies I'd had.

"No," I said. "Don't stop."

I wriggled against his hold to reinforce my request, using my entire body to fight him. Before I'd been keeping back. Now, I struggled with all I had.

Donovan fought harder too, but only with enough strength to just overcome me. He wrapped his arm around my waist, sliding my shirt up so he touched bare skin. I elbowed him in the ribs. His knee grazed against my inner thigh. Could he tell how wet I was through my leggings?

When he had me captured again, one arm behind me, one across my chest, he suddenly pushed me back until I was pinned against a bookshelf.

I gazed down to where his lower body met mine. Pressed hard at my belly was the firm bulge of his erection.

I'd long forgotten why I'd come here.

When I looked up again, his eyes were waiting. "I could smell you on his fingers."

I barely had time to wish his mouth was on mine before it was.

There was nothing tentative or easy about the way that Donovan Kincaid kissed. The pressure of his lips was firm and intent. His tongue was thick as it dipped inside, tasting me in long licks. He dropped my arms and with one hand held my face at my chin, sort of cradling it, and it felt sweet, but also like it was meant to hold me in place. So he could kiss me how he wanted. So he could suck my top lip until it was fat. So he could nip along my neck while I wriggled against him.

My knees could barely hold me. I couldn't breathe because I wanted him so much. I threw one arm around his neck, needing to hold on to something. Needing to hold on to *him*. His kiss got deeper as if he liked the way I clutched on to him. Then meaner—pulling roughly at my lip with his teeth while pinching my nipple with his fingers—as if he wished he didn't like it like he did.

His lips never left mine, but I was very aware as his hand slid down my side and under the band of my leggings, under my panties, past the hood of skin to find my clit.

My breath hitched, and he slipped deeper, through the soft curls, burrowing inside me.

"Was this how he did it?" he said, pulling away. I don't know if he wanted to watch the reaction to his question or to what he was doing.

"Yes." It was mechanically the same. Two fingers stroking my sensitive inner walls.

But it was also nothing at all the same. I was so wet. And it felt so good. So fucking good. Like kindling catching on fire, spreading heat, growing hotter. Burning. Blazing. "Donovan," I moaned.

"Say it again," he growled.

"Donovan." I'd said it so many times in the dark, in my head. It felt new to say it out loud in this way but comfortable, like finding a pair of jeans that seemed to have been perfectly tailored.

His lip turned up, the closest thing to a smile that I'd ever seen him give. Damn, his face was really striking. I'd never seen it this close up. Not pretty but captivating. He was only twenty-two and yet he already had lines starting at his eyes. His thick brows and the deep line in his chin gave him a rugged appeal, and the way he studied me while he rubbed and kneaded me below was intense and committed and...god, what he was doing to me...I closed my eyes as the pleasure built toward a climax.

"Did you touch him?" he asked, suddenly withdrawing his hand.

I opened my eyes. "No."

"Touch me." It was the same way he'd told me to sit when I'd first arrived. Then it had pissed me off to be ordered around. Now I was so eager, my hands were shaking.

Donovan caressed my face and kissed along my forehead while I worked to get his black trousers open. When I got his pants and boxer briefs worked down to the top of his muscular thighs, his cock fell out, long and thick and hard. His tip was purple and stretched tight, and all of a sudden I knew that this was going to be *it*. This was going to happen. This was going to be inside me because there was a cyclone of want blustering at the core of me, begging me to have him. But also, it *had* to happen because I had a very real fear that whatever this strange, complicated thing was that was going on with Donovan might never happen again if it didn't happen *now*.

I skimmed my palm across his crown, reverently, then drew my fingers closed around him and pulled down.

He hissed, and my stomach flipped.

Donovan brought his hand to join mine—the one slick with my wetness—and together we stroked up, down. Up. Down.

Up.

He pulled his hand away, but I kept working him, even though I could feel his eyes on me, watching me. *Asking* me.

I didn't look up. Because I didn't want to be asked, and I didn't want this to stop. And that made me an awful person and an awful woman and probably someone who needed to schedule an appointment with a campus psychiatrist as soon as possible, but so be it. *This* was my consent. I was touching him.

He seemed to understand because then he was pulling out his wallet, tearing open a condom, pushing my hand away and rolling it over his erection. Or maybe he was never asking my permission, after all.

I shimmied my leggings and panties down to my knees. Donovan lifted me and they fell to my ankles. I widened my knees, giving him room. He lined his head at my entrance and, without any hesitation, drove inside.

It hurt at first. A lot.

I was too tight and too dry, even as wet as I was. Donovan was persistent, though, pushing and nudging until I opened up for him and he could slide all the way in. Tears fell down my cheeks and my nails dug into his back. Fluid trickled past where we were joined and down my leg. I felt tense and wound up and unbridled.

But then there was Donovan's mouth, kissing me, centering me. He was just as demanding as before. Greedy and impatient like his cock. But as I gave in to his lips, my body relaxed, and soon there was no more pain, just pleasure coiling inside me, tightening and expanding.

He noticed when I gave in. I could feel his attack change. He hitched me up higher so the angle of his pelvis was better against mine and ground into me repeatedly with deep, merciless jabs. I tried to speak, to say his name, but all that came out was grunts and groans and incoherent syllables.

I was lost to him.

The shelf behind me cut into my lower back and my phone buzzed in my coat pocket on the floor by the desk and I had an F on my paper and the door to the office was unlocked and I had a date with Weston, but all I cared about in the world at the moment was the dirty, filthy scenario I was living out. It was everything I'd imagined those nights in my room—a little bit cruel and a little bit hard—plus as erotic as hell. And the man knew how to touch me. Knew how to move inside me.

It was also more. Because I'd never once imagined that, while he did those terrible sexy things, Donovan would look at me the way he looked at me. Studying my face. Watching my eyes. Like he cared about what he'd find there.

I'd never once imagined that I'd *want* that from him.

I came without warning. I'd always been finicky when it came to orgasms—my high school boyfriend had found it hard to make me come with his tongue and fingers. I'd had better luck on my own, depending on my mindset. Maybe I was a girl who needed penetration. Maybe I was a girl who needed Donovan.

He regarded me even closer as I spiraled. I fought to keep my eyes open so I could watch him watching me. He seemed to find this funny because he chuckled, kissed me again, and then plowed into me with renewed fervor.

He came on a long low grunt, and for just a moment at the end, he closed his eyes, and I'd never seen his face so relaxed. We were still catching our breath, he was still inside me, and I brought my hand up to touch his cheek—how young he looked now. How innocent.

He caught my hand against his jaw. His eyes flew open. "I didn't want to notice you," he said so quietly it was almost a whisper. "And now I don't know how not to."

Another cryptic Donovan statement, but this one made my chest feel warm and stretched. "Then notice me," I said.

He considered me a moment longer. Then stepped away, pulling out of me. "I can't."

He motioned for me to stay where I was. Then he

removed his condom, tied it off, wrapped it in tissue from the desk and pocketed it before fastening his pants. I had to give him credit—it was probably not a good idea to leave a used condom in Mr. Velasquez's office. Next Donovan brought some tissue and knelt down in front of me so he could clean up the blood and cum that had dripped down my thigh.

Then he left me with my pants still down and went to sit behind his desk.

I dressed myself and watched him, curious as he opened up his laptop and clicked a few keys. "You have an A on that paper now, Sabrina," he said, his voice not entirely steady. "I believe that should be acceptable to you." He couldn't look at me.

Dread started gathering in my stomach. "That's not. That's not why I did that." He didn't believe that. He *couldn't*. He felt bad now—as he should—and was fixing his mistake. Surely that was what this was.

"I'm sure it's not why you did that." He was more in control of himself now. He shut the laptop and finally met my eyes. "But now you'll have a chance with Weston King, won't you?"

It was a punch to the stomach. The cruelest thing he could have said.

With tears in my eyes, I grabbed my coat off the floor and started for the door. My hand was on the knob when he added, "Oh, that's right. I forgot to mention, Weston *does* like virgins. My bad."

There were a lot of words I wanted to unleash on him, but even if I tried at the moment, I knew it would come out in nothing but snot and drivel. He'd worn me down. I'd played his game and he'd won.

I opened the door and ran until I was out of the building. Ran until I couldn't run any more because I was sobbing too hard to go on. I stopped at the river to cry and catch my breath and silence my dang phone, which had been going off nonstop in my pocket.

I pulled out my cell and looked at my notifications through bleary eyes—four missed calls and several texts, all from my sister.

Aubrey: Where are you?

Aubrey: Call me ASAP. It's Dad. He's in the hospital.

Aubrey: Sabrina! It's a heart attack.

Aubrey: He's going to die. Call me. I need you.

EPILOGUE

TEN YEARS LATER

Ashley tapped her toe, anxious for the server to come by again. "I swear to god, if we don't get out of here in time because of that damn waitress..."

"Calm down, would you? It's really not that big of a deal if I don't see him." I finished the last swallow of my martini and pushed my glass aside.

"Are you kidding me? It's been—what? Ten years since you left Harvard?"

"About that." *Ten years.* It was strange how it hadn't felt like that much time had passed. It still felt like yesterday, and it also felt like it happened in another lifetime, to somebody else.

"You *have* to see him. You never got to explain to him what happened. What if he's been pining for you all this time? And he never knew that your father died. He just figured you ran off and didn't care. Though I still don't understand why you didn't just take Audrey back to Cambridge with you."

"I've been over this already," I sighed.

She threw her hands up in the air, her exasperation with

our server translating into exasperation with me. "You had a *full ride*! How could you let that slip through your fingers? I've heard you talk about the jobs you pined for—running big corporations on Wall Street and making the big bucks. You could have had that if you'd stayed!"

"I know! And believe me, I tried. But my scholarship was taken away when I didn't finish out the semester. I couldn't afford Harvard without that." It had crushed me. Almost as much as the death of my father. All my life I'd worked for that scholarship, then to have it yanked away... It was salt on a very deep open wound.

Ashley, ever true to justice, became indignant. "I know, I know. They took it away. You should have appealed it."

I'd explained this part to her before too. Many times. Something she'd probably remember if she hadn't just finished three vodka tonics in less than an hour. "I did appeal it. But the scholarship was privately funded through the MADAR Foundation and since it wasn't sponsored through the university, the donor didn't have to adhere to school policies. Blah blah blah." The memory was bitter in my mouth, months of writing letters only to be rejected time and time again. "If I'd had the right name, the right connections. If I'd had money, I'm sure things would have been different."

"Isn't that everyone's story? Hey, waitress!" she practically yelled across the bar.

"Ashley! Shh!" I didn't know why I was shushing her now. The whole restaurant was already looking at us.

She didn't mind the attention. "We made eye contact. It's cool. She saw me. She's bringing the ticket." She stole the olive from my empty martini glass. "Anyway, you got your masters at Colorado University and then got swept up by a headhunter for one of the best ad firms in California, moved to L.A., met me and your life really began. You're welcome."

I pretended to roll my eyes, but honestly, Ashley had become a great friend and confidante. Other than my sister, she was the only person I'd ever told about Donovan Kincaid and Weston King. I'd left out details both times I'd shared the story, however. No one needed to know how sick and dirty I'd been back then. With Donovan.

I still thought about him, sometimes. At night. When I couldn't sleep. When I was restless and couldn't figure out what I needed. Sometimes it was just my hand and fantasies of him.

I wasn't admitting that, though. What kind of girl still dreamed about the asshole who'd taken her virginity and thrown her aside like that?

What would have happened if I'd been able to stay?

"Here you go," the waitress said, dropping off our ticket.

She was already off to another table when Ashley caught her by the arm and pulled her back. "And here's my card. Could you hurry please? We have to be somewhere."

"We really don't," I said, but the server was already out of earshot.

"Yes, we do!" Ashley turned the "Advertising in a New Age" program around so it was facing me and pointed at the keynote speaker excitedly. "He probably thinks you stood him up all those years ago. You have to make it right!"

I stared at the program. It was still open to the page that had started this whole conversation and caused us to miss two panels already.

His picture showed he'd aged well.

But I already knew that. I'd seen both of their pictures many times, and they'd both aged well. Weston King and Donovan Kincaid were famous in the ad world. Instead of following Harvard with jobs in their fathers' investment firm, they'd opened up an international advertising agency. Weston ran the office in the States and Donovan ran the branch in Tokyo.

When I'd agreed to go to New York for three days with Ashley for this conference, I'd had no idea he'd be a speaker.

"He probably won't even remember me," I said, staring at his panty-melting dimple.

"Who could forget you? With a face like his, I'd use any card I had to try to get close to him. He's a hottie. Oh, wait, I forgot you're more into brains than looks these days—maybe he'll share all his award-winning inspirations with an old friend."

I shook my head and pulled my hand through my hair—the ponytail was long gone, but the habit was not. I probably should see his speech anyway. And what was the harm in sticking around afterward? Wouldn't it be nice to finally have some closure to those days?

The waitress returned with the bill and Ashley quickly signed.

"All right," Ashley said. "Ready, Bri?"

It was a loaded question. Was anyone ever ready for men like Weston King and Donovan Kincaid?

Pulling out my phone, I used the camera to freshen up my lipstick and took a deep breath. "Let's do this."

Ready for more? You can pre-order Dirty Filthy Rich Men now.

Up next for Laurelin Paige, with Sierra Simone, Hot Cop!

LET'S STAY IN TOUCH!

Join my fan group, The Sky Launch, at www.facebook.com/groups/HudsonPierce

Like my author page at www.facebook.com/LaurelinPaige

Sign up for my newsletter where you'll receive a FREE book every month from bestselling authors, only available to my subscribers, as well as up-to-date information on my latest releases.

Visit www.laurelinpaige.com to find out more about me and all my books.

ALSO BY LAURELIN PAIGE

The Dirty Universe

Dirty Filthy Rich Men (Dirty Duet #1) (March 27, 2017)

Dirty Filthy Rich Love (Dirty Duet #2) (September 11, 2017)

Dirty Filthy Fix (a spinoff novella) (November 7, 2017)

Dirty Sexy Player (a spinoff novel) (Early 2018)

The Fixed Universe

Fixed on You (Fixed #1)

Found in You (Fixed #2)

Forever with You (Fixed #3)

Fixed Trilogy Bundle (all three Fixed books in one bundle)

Hudson (a companion novel)

Free Me (a spinoff novel – Found duet #1)

Find Me (Found duet #2)

Chandler (a spinoff novel)

Falling Under You (a spinoff novella)

First and Last

First Touch

Last Kiss

Written with Kayti McGee under the name Laurelin McGee

Hot Alphas

Miss Match

Love Struck

Written with Sierra Simone

Porn Star

Hot Cop (Coming Summer 2017!)

ABOUT THE AUTHOR

Laurelin Paige is the *NY Times, Wall Street Journal,* and *USA Today* Bestselling Author of the Fixed Trilogy. She's a sucker for a good romance and gets giddy any time there's kissing, much to the embarrassment of her three daughters. Her husband doesn't seem to complain, however. When she isn't reading or writing sexy stories, she's probably singing, watching *Game of Thrones* and *The Walking Dead*, or dreaming of Michael Fassbender. She's also a proud member of Mensa International, though she doesn't do anything with the organization except use it as material for her bio.

Find me online
www.laurelinpaige.com
laurelinpaigeauthor@gmail.com